Katie Woo's

✳ Neighborhood ✳

Good Morning,
Farmer Carmen!

by Fran Manushkin

illustrated by Laura Zarrin

PICTURE WINDOW BOOKS
a capstone imprint

Katie Woo's Neighborhood is published by
Picture Window Books, an imprint of Capstone.
1710 Roe Crest Drive
North Mankato, Minnesota 56003
www.capstonepub.com

Text © 2020 by Fran Manushkin.
Illustrations © 2020 by Capstone.

Cataloging-in-Publication Data is available on the
Library of Congress website.
ISBN: 978-1-5158-4815-8 (library binding)
ISBN: 978-1-5158-5875-1 (paperback)
ISBN: 978-1-5158-4819-6 (eBook PDF)

Summary: Katie learns what a vegetable farmer does when she visits a farm and helps sell the vegetables at a farmers market.

Graphic Designer: Bobbie Nuytten

Printed and bound in the USA.
PA100

Table of Contents

Katie's Neighborhood

Police

Library

Mechanic

City Hall

Grocery Store

Post Office

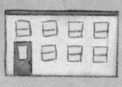

Chapter 1
Is It Fun to be a Farmer?

In the summer, Katie and her friends loved going to the farmers market.

Every Sunday they found new foods to taste.

"Come and meet my aunt Carmen," said Pedro. "She's a new farmer at the market."

"Hi!" said Katie. "Is it fun to be a farmer?"

"You can find out," said Aunt Carmen. "Come and stay overnight next Saturday. You can help bring my veggies to market."

"That's cool!" said Katie.

"I'm wild about tomatoes.

Maybe I can help pick them."

"For sure," said Farmer

Carmen.

Chapter 2
The Tasty Farm

On Saturday morning,

Pedro's dad drove Katie

and JoJo and Pedro to Aunt

Carmen's farm. It was a

long ride.

"Welcome!" called Farmer
Carmen. "Let me show you
around."

Katie saw long, long rows
of lettuce and purple and
green cabbages.

"Uh-oh," said Katie.

"I don't see tomatoes."

"Don't worry," said
Farmer Carmen. "They are
over here. Pick a big one
and take a bite."

"Wow!" Katie shouted.

"It's juicy, juicy, JUICY!"

Aunt Carmen smiled.

"My tomatoes passed the

test. They are perfect for

market tomorrow."

Pedro joked, "These cucumbers have goose bumps. They must be cold."

Katie joked back, "They are excited about going to market."

Katie and JoJo helped

Farmer Carmen pick tomatoes.

Pedro liked picking peppers.

He also liked saying, "Pedro is

picking peppers" over and over.

Dinner was a tasty salad.

"Let's go to bed early,"

said Farmer Carmen. "We

must wake up at four a.m.

to pack up my veggies to

take to market."

Chapter 3
Farmers Market Day

It was still dark when

Katie woke up. She saw

Farmer Carmen and her

helpers packing veggies

into baskets. They loaded

the baskets onto the truck.

Katie saw the sunrise

as they rode to market.

She yawned and yawned.

"I don't think farmers sleep

very much," she said.

At the market, JoJo and Pedro stacked up cabbages. Katie tucked tomatoes into pretty baskets.

Pedro said, "Aunt Carmen

works so hard. I hope we sell

everything."

"We will," said Katie.

But she was a little worried.

There was so much to sell!

Miss Winkle wanted lots of tomatoes.

Katie told her, "I picked some and packed them."

"Way to go!" said Miss Winkle.

Katie sold carrots to Sharon, the mail carrier. Mr. Nelson got lettuce and cabbage for his grocery store.

But at closing time, many

veggies weren't sold.

"This is sad," said Pedro.

"Very sad!" said JoJo.

"Wait!" yelled Katie.

"Look who's coming?"

It was Haley O'Hara and her five brothers and sisters.

"Yay!" yelled Haley. "We're not too late for veggies."

They filled seven bags.

No veggies were left!

Katie told Farmer Carmen,
"You work very hard!"

"But my work is tasty,"
said Farmer Carmen. They
shared the last tomato.

It was very tasty!

Glossary

cabbage (KAB-ij)—a large vegetable with green or purple leaves shaped into a round head

cucumber (KYOO-kuhm-bur)—a long, green vegetable with a soft center filled with seeds

farmers market (FAR-mers MAR-kit)—a shopping area where people sell the items they grow

lettuce (LET-iss)—a green, leafy salad vegetable

tomato (tuh-MAY-toh)—a red, juicy fruit eaten as a vegetable either raw or cooked

Katie's Questions

1. What traits make a good farmer? Would you like to be a farmer? Why or why not?

2. In the first chapter, Katie asks Farmer Carmen if it is fun to be a farmer. Does Farmer Carmen think farming is fun? What about Katie? Do you think it would be fun to be a farmer?

3. When Katie says she is wild about tomatoes, what does she mean?

4. List as many vegetables as you can. How many did you list? Which one is your favorite?

5. Imagine you have your own stand at a farmers market. What would you sell? Draw a picture of your farmers market stand.

Katie Interviews Farmer Carmen

Katie: Hi, Farmer Carmen! Thanks for talking to me about being a farmer. I'm curious . . . what do you like best about being a farmer?

Farmer Carmen: As you know, Katie, there are so many great things about being a farmer. I love working outside in the fresh air and sunshine. And I love working with my hands. But the thing I love best is growing food that feeds people in my community and beyond.

Katie: How do farmers decide what to grow?

Farmer Carmen: The plants we grow need to be right for the climate. That means how hot it usually is and how much rain we get. Some plants need lots of sunshine. Others grow better in cooler places. But not all farmers grow things.

Katie: If they aren't growing things, what do they do?

Farmer Carmen: They raise things! The animals that farmers raise are called livestock. Some livestock is raised for meat, and some is raised for the things they give us.

Katie: What do you mean "give us"?
Farmer Carmen: Like chickens give us eggs, and sheep give us wool.

Katie: And cows give us milk!
Farmer Carmen: You got it, Katie. You catch on so fast. You'd make a great farmer.

Katie: Thanks! So, what would I need to do if I decided that I wanted to be a farmer for real?
Farmer Carmen: Most farmers are trained by working on farms. There's no better way to learn, if you ask me. Some people study farming at college too.

Katie: Well, thanks again for talking to me. And big thanks for working so hard to feed all of us! You are the best!
Farmer Carmen: Thanks, Katie. I think you are pretty great too!

About the Author

Fran Manushkin is the author of Katie Woo, the highly acclaimed fan-favorite early-reader series, as well as the popular Pedro series. Her other books include *Happy in Our Skin*, *Baby, Come Out!* and

the best-selling board books *Big Girl Panties* and *Big Boy Underpants*. There is a real Katie Woo: Fran's great-niece, who doesn't get into trouble like the Katie in the books. Fran lives in New York City, three blocks from Central Park, where she can often be found bird-watching and daydreaming. She writes at her dining room table, without the help of her two naughty cats, Chaim and Goldy.

About the Illustrator

Laura spent her early childhood in the St. Louis, Missouri, area. There she explored creeks, woods, and attic closets, climbed trees, and dug for artifacts in the backyard, all in preparation for her future career as an archeologist. She never became one, however, because she realized she's much happier drawing in the comfort of her own home while watching TV. When she was twelve, her family moved to the Silicon Valley in California, where she still resides with her very logical husband and teen sons, and their illogical dog, Cody.